The Naughty Puppy

First published in 2001 by
Franklin Watts
96 Leonard Street
London
EC2A 4XD

Franklin Watts Australia
45-51 Huntley Street
Alexandria
NSW 2015

A CIP catalogue record for this book is available from the British Library.

ISBN 0 7496 3930 X (hbk)
ISBN 0 7496 4383 8 (pbk)

Series Editor: Louise John
Series Advisor: Dr Barrie Wade
Series Designer: Jason Anscomb

Printed in China

The Naughty Puppy

by Jillian Powell

Illustrated by Summer Durantz

W
FRANKLIN WATTS
LONDON•SYDNEY

It was the day of the dog show.

Gemma took her puppy, Barney.

But Barney was a very naughty puppy.

Everyone walked their puppy around the judging ring.

4
5
6

All the puppies followed their owners ...

... except Barney, who chased a butterfly.

Everyone told their puppy to sit and they all sat ...

... except Barney, who rolled in the grass.

Everyone told their puppy to stay and they all stayed ...

... except Barney, who wanted to play.

Then all of the puppies had to fetch sticks.

Barney fetched the judge's umbrella instead.

The judge was very cross!

Gemma was cross, too.

"You're a very naughty puppy," she told Barney.

Suddenly, the wind blew the judge's hat off.

It blew up in the air and away.

Everyone stood and watched ...

... except Barney, who chased the big, red hat.

“Catch it, Barney!”
everyone shouted.

Barney jumped up and
caught the hat.

The judge was very pleased.
"Well done, Barney!"
she said.

Barney wagged his tail proudly.

The judge gave Barney a special prize for being the cleverest puppy in the show!

Leapfrog has been specially designed to fit the requirements of the National Literacy Strategy. It offers real books for beginning readers by top authors and illustrators.

There are 25 Leapfrog stories to choose from:

The Bossy Cockerel

Written by Margaret Nash,
illustrated by Elisabeth Moseng

Bill's Baggy Trousers

Written by Susan Gates,
illustrated by Anni Axworthy

Mr Spotty's Potty

Written by Hilary Robinson,
illustrated by Peter Utton

Little Joe's Big Race

Written by Andy Blackford,
illustrated by Tim Archbold

The Little Star

Written by Deborah Nash,
illustrated by Richard Morgan

The Cheeky Monkey

Written by Anne Cassidy,
illustrated by Lisa Smith

Selfish Sophie

Written by Damian Kelleher,
illustrated by Georgie Birkett

Recycled!

Written by Jillian Powell,
illustrated by Amanda Wood

Felix on the Move

Written by Maeve Friel,
illustrated by Beccy Blake

Pippa and Poppa

Written by Anne Cassidy,
illustrated by Philip Norman

Jack's Party

Written by Ann Bryant,
illustrated by Claire Henley

The Best Snowman

Written by Margaret Nash,
illustrated by Jörg Saupe

Eight Enormous Elephants

Written by Penny Dolan,
illustrated by Leo Broadley

Mary and the Fairy

Written by Penny Dolan,
illustrated by Deborah Allwright

The Crying Princess

Written by Anne Cassidy,
illustrated by Colin Paine

Cinderella

Written by Barrie Wade,
illustrated by Julie Monks

The Three Little Pigs

Written by Maggie Moore,
illustrated by Rob Hefferan

The Three Billy Goats Gruff

Written by Barrie Wade,
illustrated by Nicola Evans

Goldilocks and the Three Bears

Written by Barrie Wade,
illustrated by Kristina Stephenson

Jack and the Beanstalk

Written by Maggie Moore,
illustrated by Steve Cox

Little Red Riding Hood

Written by Maggie Moore,
illustrated by Paula Knight

Jasper and Jess

Written by Anne Cassidy,
illustrated by François Hall

The Lazy Scarecrow

Written by Jillian Powell,
illustrated by Jayne Coughlin

The Naughty Puppy

Written by Jillian Powell,
illustrated by Summer Durantz

Freddie's Fears

Written by Hilary Robinson,
illustrated by Ross Collins